LIFE & LOVE

In The Key of B

IVORY KEYS

PUBLISHING
WWW.SWAYEDLOTUSDESIGNS.COM
Email: divinelyswampublishing@gmail.com

Dedicated to:

All the women in the world who has a best friend and you are holding one another down like sisters.
& To the Memory of McDaniel (Scoop) Smith III R.I.P.

"Having at least one sister that you can count on is better than a thousand friends you can't trust."

~*Ivory Keys*

ABOUT LIFE & LOVE

I've been going to his establishment for over a year.

Flirting, winking, blowing kisses and he stills acts as if I don't exist.

Then, Saturday night happened...

I was locked in his embrace.

I discovered that there was no place on earth I would rather be than in his arms.

However, he asks me a question.

I didn't answer as he felt I should, so he broke my heart.

He's left me nursing broken pieces with lingering memories of our heated night.

Meanwhile, my best friend is moving on with her life and a new love.

And I realize one thing for sure...

Life is hard all by itself, and when you add love to the equation, it can very well become a problem.

But I heard, all is fair in Life & Love.

CHAPTER 1
I NEED TO FIND MYSELF

MACY

I pull my hair into a ponytail and adjust the elastic band to keep it from pulling too tight. Today is that day—clean up day and the last thing I need is for my freshly done hair to be sweeping through dust.

Although cleaning isn't what I want to be doing, it's definitely what's needed. Looking around my home causes me to think how this girl prayed for something I don't even have the time to love or make love in. I sleep, poop, and eat here, but still haven't had the chance to relax in it like the queen who signed those mortgage papers.

In reality, everyone hopes to have a spot filled with love, life, and joy. And let's not forget a whole lot of sex. Instead, mine is filled with dust, unwatched televisions, unopened boxes, and a whole lot of potential.

If I had a choice, I'd be snuggled up under a fine man who radiates in the scent of a man who wants to impress a woman. Unfortunately, I don't have one of those either or can't even foresee one in the near future. Not because I don't want that, but because I'm so locked down in debt that taking care of me is definitely on the back burner. Also, the one I've been eyeing, isn't checking for me.

As soon as the music begins to play, I twirl to the soulful sound of Kem's soothing voice blazing through the speakers. My size sixteen hips sway from side to side as this broom dance gives me life. There is nothing like having a Saturday clean up day grooving to music that makes you want to move.

Something I learned from my mother.

Cleaning always comes easier when you are on the phone chatting it up about something worth talking about, or listening to music that makes you move, groove, and dance. Just a little life lesson my momma taught me that I will never forget.

After I finish sweeping the kitchen, I plop down on the stool in front of the island with the broom still in my hand.

"Macy J, it's time to get your life girl."

Whatever that meant.

I will be the first to say that I don't even have a clue. It actually just sounds good because at this point, I am a thirty-six year old woman who does not know what in the hell I'm supposed to be doing or want to do. You would think that by now, I would have my life all together, working in a career that I love, living with a man who is loving me, and making enough coins to be able to go to the grocery store and buy whatever my eyes see and hands touch.

None of that is my reality.

Instead, I'm working as a secretary to a man who neither appreciates or respects me. How do I know? My pay is just enough to keep me from sinking and he has no intention of giving me one dime over what he feels I deserve. Which is exactly why I stopped acting like superwoman.

When I started the job, I was so happy to be employed that I cleaned the office like it was my house. Cooking and shit, bringing his ass lunch like I was feeding my man, and even taking out trash. A fucking unpaid susie homemaker. Lately, the only thing outside of answering the phone I care to do is open the mail. Believe me, I only enjoy that because I like being nosey.

The only perk to being on the job is working side by side with my best friend and sister, Josephine. You know, work always feels better when you are going to hang out with someone you really like or love. She's my girl and when all the chips go down, I know I can count on her.

Okay, girl, it's time to get up and get back to moving.

I put the broom in the broom closet and closed the door because I don't plan on using it any more.

What is next, Macy?

I turn around toward the sink, loaded with dishes. My next chore. I'm washing these damn dishes but at the same time making a mental note to buy some paper plates, cups, and utensils, since it's only me and I have no one to be fancy for or with.

By the time Maze flows through the speakers, I know exactly what I need. I need to be out amongst some people who are just as needy as me. Hopefully, something that will help me discover myself is lurking and waiting on me.

The Sugar Shack!

"Sumthin' Sumthin" by Maxwell pours through the speakers.

I thrust my pelvic, and then drop down into a twerk, come back up and wiggle my butt in what I've termed my catch-em-trap-em move.

"Oh it's on tonight!"

I need to find myself, and get back to doing the things that make me happy. I also need to put all of these stressors behind me and think about how to come up financially without losing my soul. Right now, The Sugar Shack is just the place I need to be to regroup, and reconnect to me.

Macy Michelle Jones, the girl who loves to dance, has a good drink every now and again, and gets with a man who wants to give himself without thinking he owns what he's getting. That part right there.

I clean up all the things I've used to clean up with and my next move is to find a bad outfit that will make somebody's son want to come home with me.

She's on a mission.

CHAPTER 2
TWO IS BETTER THAN ONE
MACY & JOSEPHINE

Going to the club has never been one of those things I've cared to do alone, and though I don't fool with too many females, there's one I can trust with my keys and my coins, my best friend, Josephine. I call her Jo for short.

I pick up the phone and dial her number, hoping and praying she ain't got nothing going on at that holier-than-heaven church she attends. I'm all for being in the presence of God but you can miss me on that twice in one week attendance.

"Answer the darn phone," I mumble and she picks up on the third ring sounding like she's just as happy to hear from me as I am that she answered the phone.

Jo giggles. "Hey, chick, what's up?"

"I just knew your ass was somewhere at the church house and I wouldn't be able to get you. Damn, I'm glad you answered this phone!" I wait for the rebuttal because I know better than to say anything negative about her church.

"Girl, I have told you to keep your mouth off my church and if I were, that still wouldn't stop me from talking to you.

What's going on, Jay?" She calls me by the nickname she's been calling me since the sixth grade.

"I want to go to The Sugar Shack tonight, and you know I ain't going by myself. You down?"

She giggles. "Like four flat tires put down by a bitch who caught her man tipping."

I holler because her crazy ass always comes up with these sayings that make me laugh as hard as I'm laughing right now. "All right so you coming by me to get dressed?"

"You know this. Momma is all up in my business enough and she'll be calling Grady asking him if we are together. Who doesn't need all that drama is me." Grady is the man she's been off and on with for five years.

"I feel you. Come on over because I figure if we get there by eight thirty, we'll be able to have the booth in the corner that we like."

"That'll work. See you later."

"Nawl, see you soon." I say this because she has a tendency to be late. We both hang up the phone and I start doing my dance again. *It's going to be a good night.* Every time Jo and I go out, we cut up.

Women are looking at us all mad and the men are looking like they wish they would have left their mad chick at the house. But I guess if it were me watching us, I'd be looking just like them. We do the most.

Both Jo and I are well endowed in the butt section and neither of us had to get injections or booty pads. God just blessed us in all the right places and everything else is snatched by the best Spanx made.

I pull my hair from the ponytail holder and shake my head until my natural curly hair falls on my shoulders. I look up at the clock.

"It's five and that means I only have three hours and it's

going to take two hours to comb my hair and beat my face. I better get started now."

The first thing I do is take a bath, because my girl—as in my vagina—has got to be smelling fresh and clean. I make sure to wash it real good and then I finish the task of cleaning everywhere else. When I'm finished bathing, I oil my body down with baby oil, and then wipe off the excess oil with my dry off towel.

"She's fresh, clean, and this melanin is popping." I'm my first and best cheerleader.

I pull out my entire makeup collection and lay what I need on the towel I've folded on the counter by the sink. Then, I pull out my lashes and my red lipstick. Trust, I have certain lashes that go with the red lipstick because the eyes must talk dirty, while the lips look luscious.

After my face is beat to perfection, I part my hair to the side, whip and section where it lays flat on my face without falling in my eyes. I pin the part I call my swoop, then brush the other side to the back to meet right at the corner where I make a messy bun in the back; but more to the side.

For the dress I intend to catch in, my hair, face, boots, and bag needs to complement each other. This style brings out a sexiness with a hint of seduction.

"It's about to be on and popping! I'll have my girl by my side and getting a man on my mind." *Well, for me, one particular man.*

At exactly six-twenty, I hear my doorbell chime. I hit the button on my phone and tell Jo to come on in and turn off the alarm. She knows my code and comes right in. I admire her outfit.

"Jo, you gonna be clean in all that damn white. What are you trying to go angel on a sister tonight?"

She laughs and continues to lay out her outfit. "Girl, I just felt a black and white movement and heck, you're right there with me in those white boots." We clap one another's hands because we both are showing thighs.

Jo does her rendition of a twerk to the music still flowing from Alexa and I fall out laughing because the girl knows how to make her ass jiggle like one of those high paid strippers. Either my ass is too firm or it didn't get the memo because I never learned how to do that.

But one thing is for sure, I'm glad I've got a friend who is built up just like me and we aren't big girls with low self-esteem. As a matter of fact, we are the prime example that two is always better than one. And when we step, we make it do what it do.

I spray some perfume on my neck, behind my ears, knees, and under my dress, just in case I run up on something that's willing to take a smell in some hidden spaces.

After we are both dressed, I look at my girl Jo. "You ready, friend."

"I was born ready, Macy J."

And in my Beyonce' voice I say, "Let's go get 'em!"

CHAPTER 3
SUGAR SHACK ON LOCK
MACY & JOSEPHINE

We walk through the doors and it's just like I knew it would be...all eyes on us.

The queens of Queensborough make an entrance to entice the sugar daddies and shake some shit up in the shack. Baby, it is crucial. The DJ fancies us with a little Maxwell and instead of walking to our seats, we groove from the door to the booth.

The grand entrance I need to set the mood.

"Just as sure as the sky is blue," I belt out the song and pop my fingers. I close my eyes, fantasizing that I'm singing to a man who looks as good as the one singing the song.

By the time I open my eyes, a couple of men at the table next to us have caught the vibes. They are looking at Jo and I like two fresh chickens that has just come off the line, been plucked, and are seasoned and ready to get cooked in their oil.

Then to make matters worse, the DJ hits us with "Baby, I'm Ready," by the late LeVert. By now, I'm up and moving my body to the beat giving the men in the table next to us a good old show.

You can best well believe, I'll give a free show, but I'll

never be a free freak. And when I started singing, the girl from the bar brings over a microphone and puts it in my hand. Now why she have to go and do that? Right in front of their very eyes, I turn into Diana with no need for background help.

By the time the song finishes, the waitress has a bowl on my table and people fills it with bills. Trust, I am taking every penny that I've earned. After my performance, men are coming up to our table asking for our numbers and shooting their best shot.

I smile but of all the men in The Sugar Shack, only one has my eye. The owner who everyone calls, Scoop. He has some smooth skin, beautiful wavy hair, and his gray eyes always do a number on me all by themselves.

I lean over and whisper to Jo, "Dang, I'm going to need him to stop looking at me like that. My panties are getting wet."

"Who?" Jo starts casing the room to see who is staring in our direction. "Gray eyes?"

"Heck, yeah." I bite my bottom lip. "Girl, his eyes are burning a flame in me and old girl is feeling pressure."

Jo giggles. "You know anything will excite that dry bush." We both burst out laughing.

It has been almost six years since I had a man between my legs doing anything and to be honest, I don't even know why I made the deal to torture myself.

That's the lie I tell.

Truth is, I stay away from sex to keep me from putting this kitty on another crazy wack job who wants to own it like it belongs to him.

The old ass man who took my virginity taught me at the age of sixteen how to please a man. I realize old school knew what he was talking about. Every young man I've had after him can hardly take the heat I gave. They either start acting a fool or try to keep tabs on me like I'm in pussy prison.

I take my focus off Scoop, so my body can stop speaking its own language.

The DJ hits us with "Slow Down" by Bobby Valentino. Jo and I are singing and acting like two loose girls who have snuck away from home and are having the best time of our lives. We are definitely changing the vibe in the place and some of the other women want in.

Too late. All eyes are being blessed with our booties. Rolling, popping, thrusting, and grooving.

Drinks start coming to our table back to back, but I have a remedy for that. A smile and a wink. However, the ice bucket in the center of our table is the makeshift sink to house all the alcoholic beverages sent by thirst buckets. Getting us drunk will not get them laid.

I catch him staring again and this time, he grins like he's been watching my trick all night...and has. So, I wink my eye at him and then turn my back. One, I don't want him to perceive me as thirsty, and two, I am never chasing a man or even giving him the notion I will.

When the song ends, Jo is deep in conversation with one of the men from the table next to ours. I side-eye his boy because I am not giving him any type of play. When it looks like he is about to build his nerves to talk to me, I politely pick up my bag and excuse myself from our table.

Shit, I just block that, cause I wouldn't let it be so. I grin walking toward the hall leading to the bathroom.

"Hey," I turn at the sound of a man's voice. "You don't ever have to use the public restroom when you come here. Go in that door right there," Gray eyes says after he clicks a button in his hand that causes the door he points at to unlock.

"Hmph. Oh, so I'm getting VIP treatment? How many women get this same privilege?" I ask because I would have been just fine using the mirror in the public restroom.

Scoop closes the gaps between us. He looks me up and

down and runs his hand down my arm. "To be honest, none. But I can only bring you to the stage if you want to be there. Do you?"

I side eye him. "It depends on what stage you're talking about and who'll be there with me."

"Girl, stop playing." He opens the door and I walk in past him and into his plush office that looks like a professional cloud. He clicks the same button and locks the door.

CHAPTER 4
TABLE TALK
JOSEPHINE

I watch Macy walk off, and I instantly turn my head to see who else is about to make a move. Normally, I don't believe in us splitting up, but because I know Scoop has his mind on Jay, I'm going to keep entertaining this dude who calls himself P-baby.

He's fine as hell and these Levi's and cowboy boots give me this vibe that he's a hard-working man. Now, I have run into some fake country boy clowns, but his conversation has been fresh and he's making me laugh, which is a huge plus.

He takes a swig of his drink without turning his eyes from me. The intensity of his stare has me adjusting in my seat. He's so easy to talk to and I know a man this sweet and kind has to have a lady somewhere. *But tonight, I'm going to pretend like he's mine.*

I lean in. "So tell me, what's on your mind?"

He smiles and I instantly know where his thoughts are. Shut, to be honest, I have been watching his thick fingers all night. If his penis is as thick as his fingers, this dude has the potential to turn me out.

As he's speaking, my mind drifts to Grady.

He's a sweet man, but Grady's in need of a D-doctor and I don't know one. He has this mushroomed shaped penis that is short, and because the head is so big it can give the facade that you are getting a big one. I work with it but every now and again, I long for the long stroke that can make my toes curl and my body spasm.

My butt is going to get enough for settling.

I lean in. "I'm sorry, what did you say?"

He rubs his hand on mine. "I said, you smell good."

I smile. "I'm a lady and smelling good comes with the territory."

With a grin that's making me feel some kind of way he says, "I wish I could smell all of you."

"Baby, you can if you say the right things and do what a man knows he should be doing." *Your butt can feel, lick, touch, grope, and "F"me.*

He grins. "Oh, and what's that?"

"My daddy always told me when a man puts his money in the place he wants his penis to go, that means he's all in. So me, I'm waiting for that man."

P-baby goes in his pocket and pulls out a money clip full of big heads.

I look at him because money hasn't ever enticed me to the point I'd give someone I've just met my vjay. He pulls ten bills from his clip and slides them over to me.

I'm tickled. "So what's this for? I hope you don't think I got a thousand dollar vjay. If that's the case then you can get this back and ain't nothing cheap about me."

"I'm just making a down payment tonight, because if things go my way, I'll be putting money wherever you need it and lacing you down with all the dick you want. Now, the easy part is giving you whatever you need. The hard part is you giving your whole self to me. The ball's in your court."

Shut, where has he been all my life?

I roll the money up and stick it in my bra with my eyes glued to him. Then I make it known. "I ain't a whore so this change didn't buy you nothing. So, what's your next move?"

"To be honest, I don't have one but since you walked in tonight, I knew I had a mission. You've danced your butt in here multiple times, entertained, and left with your girl. My mission is for you to leave with me."

This time I'm the one taking a drink. I furrow my brow and ask, "And what exactly would you do with me—if and when—you've accomplished your mission?"

He smiles. "Take the angel home with me and show her what it feels like to be treated like one. Then make sure you know that ain't no leaving once you are in."

I grin. "Slow your roll, homeboy. Your mission could turn out to be my mistake."

He grins and drinks the rest of his Remy and coke.

The DJ starts playing, "Focus" by H.E.R. and he pulls me from my seat and into his arms. I love a man who can dance and by the way this dude is moving his body, he's my kind of guy. His big hands grip my butt, but in a sensitive way that makes me feel more like his lady than a woman he's trying to bang.

Damn! This dude is playing hardball. I lay my body into him more, feeling somewhat like I'm at home in his arms. He smells like Creed. I'd know that smell from any scent because it's the one our boss, John, wears.

But what about Grady, Jo? What about the man who really does love you with every ounce of his soul?

I talk back to my thoughts. What about, Jo? What about the woman who needs a full package more than she wants a promise?

P-baby leans down and whispers in my ear, "Josephine, just let me have one night with you and you'll never have to 'F' with me again unless it's your choice."

"But I don't even know your real name."

He twirls me out and then brings me back to him. *Heck, I'm feeling like Cinderella at the ball.*

"My name is Philip Micheals, and I own Micheals and Sons Construction on Highway 1. I'm thirty-nine, have never been married, don't have any children, but I'm believing in God for a wife. My birthday is December the third, my driver's license number is 004617228 and I live off Ellerbe Road at 3218 Jennifer Lane in a two story home that I'll take you to if you let me."

Dayumm! I ain't ever had a man go deep on me like this. "I can't leave without telling Macy where I'm going."

"That's fine, we'll wait on her to get back, but my boy Scoop has been watching Macy for a full year and if he's with her right now, it's Christmas in June for him."

CHAPTER 5
SWEET HEAT IN THE SHACK
MACY & SCOOP

D ang, he has locked me in his office and I can't trust anything right now. I swallow because the anticipation of the moment is already getting the best of me. This man is over six feet tall, built to perfection, and I've been lusting after him for an entire year. But how far am I willing to go? All roads seem to be leading to pure ecstasy and fantasy filled delights. But the freak died a long time ago.

I look around admiring the white furniture as "Focus" by H.E.R. fills the atmosphere.

He walks behind me, pulls me into his body with one arm, and before I can react, we are swaying as he sings in my ear. It feels good to be in the arms of a man and it doesn't hurt that I can feel his penis, hard, and all up on my butt and the bottom of my back. That means one thing...my butt up against him is turning him on. *At least I'm not by myself...horny and secretly begging for affection.*

We sway as if we've been connected by love, but that's just in my fantasy. Then he twirls and guides our bodies until my back is against the wall and his lips are on my neck. *Rough house me then, but I'm glad he knows how. But don't do too much because it will knock me right out of sexy into boxer.*

He whispers, "Tell me what you want," and the heat of his breath sends chills through me.

At this point, I don't know my dang self. I close my eyes, and bite my bottom lip-my nervous habit-because just having him this close to me is literally blowing my mind.

I've been coming here for a whole year. Staring in his face, and sometimes he acted as if he was not in the least bit interested. I've been feening for and even dreaming about him. And now, he's got me locked in his office and he's asking me what I want. A ring, house, and the title of being your wife! I gotta flip this.

I release my lip and make a tender smacking noise. "No, Scoop, you tell me what you want."

He lets his tongue roam from the top of my ear to the middle of my neck, then he says, "Right now, all I want is you."

My vjay is thumping so hard I feel she might jump out my panties and purr. My breathing is shallow and intense, and he puts his tongue in my mouth and explores it with ease.

I want this man!

I pull him in and suck his tongue like I've been wishing I could for a whole year. It feels good to him because the harder I pull, the more he presses. By the time I make a groaning sound, his hand has found its way into my panties. Scoop is stroking my girl in the right place, causing my body to do something I thought it had forgotten how...react.

I moan and he sticks his finger in my passion place, brings it out, and sucks the juice off his finger.

I can feel him staring at me and all he says as he uses his hand to drive me wild is, "Open your eyes and look at me, Macy Jay."

I opened my eyes, but my head went back. I'm losing my

mind. The panting sound coming from me is getting deeper as my vjay gets wetter. F! Ssssuuuus! F!

He's all in my face, but his finger is shaking my clit so fast until it feels like a human vibrator. With authority he says, "Talk to me Macy. Tell me what you want from me."

"Uhhh, uhhh," I moan. "Screw me. I want you to screw me!"

I thought he would pull out his penis. Instead, he drops to his knees, puts one of my legs on his shoulder, and begins sucking the place he's just finished rubbing.

I feel like I am outside of myself but when I look over my shoulder at the mirror, it is definitely me. No matter how I try, I can't keep my mouth from making sounds. He is messing me up with his tongue and with one flick and two pulls, an orgasm shoots through me like I've never experienced before.

He sucks until my entire body shakes from the after shock. Then he puts his tongue in my vjay and savors my sweet heat.

He stands up and I look into his eyes. He messed me all up and didn't even use his penis. I gotta have more of him. *I want it all.*

"Are you ready to tell me what you want?"

This time, I call Scoop by his government name. "Samuel, I want you. Is that too much to ask?"

He looks deep into my eyes. "Macy, it's not, but I don't think you're ready for what you are asking for."

Now you're a mind reader? How the hell do you know what I'm ready for? That's what I wanted to say. Instead, I fix my clothes and make sure that I look just as presentable as I did when I came through his door.

He said what he said–but all I heard in what he said was–he isn't ready to give me anything beyond a wet hot experience. However, at this junction in my life, I'm independent enough to use my vibrator for pleasure without commitment. No, thanks.

I smile because if it's one thing I know, you can't taste a

little of Macy Jay and not want more. When he comes back begging, I'll be the one holding the gun. "Thank you for the experience, now would you please unlock the door."

Without saying a word, he picks up the key fob from the table, mashes a button, and I hear the door unlock. It's time for me to get my butt out of The Sugar Shack and into my shower.

The only problem is, I will never be able to wash what just happened from my mind anytime soon.

Back to the basics.

CHAPTER 6
THE PAIN FROM PLEASURE
JOSEPHINE

Although P-baby has my attention, I still keep looking at the door my girl walked through on her way to the restroom. Surely, she should be back by now, but Scoop is also still missing in action. From what his boy said, he is just as needy for Jay's affection as she is for him.

But still, she'd been back there much longer than I cared for her to be.

"Hey, P-baby, I think I need to go check on Jay."

"Josephine, Jay's a grown woman who is probably doing what I want to be doing to you."

Uh hum. Let 'em talk long enough and a fool will tell you exactly what's on his heart. "So you say."

I pull myself from his arms, and just as I am about to pick up my bag, Macy comes walking toward me, but I can't tell if she's hurt or mad.

"Jo, I'm ready to go."

I look at her to make sure she ain't been hit. I don't carry this forty-five for nothing and if I have to use it, I will; especially behind my girl.

I pull Macy by the arm. "Did he do something to you?"

A tear falls from her eyes. "I just need to go now."

I take Macy by the hand and lead her toward the front door.

"Say, Jo, can I call you?"

"I'll hit you later, P-baby. Remember I got your card."

I hear him say, "Damn, Scoop dune messed up my night."

I giggled because little does he know, he f'ed up his own night when he acted as if he didn't care about my girl. Macy is the closest thing I have to a sister and to throw me off from checking on her is to put your behind in my face as well.

"Give me the keys," I say to Macy when we make it to her car. "I'll drive because you are apparently in no shape to drive me anywhere."

She does as I've asked and we both get in the car. We ride in complete silence because I know she needs time to process whatever had happened. I warned her over and over that a man as fine as Scoop is dangerous, but he's had her nose wide open since the first time we met him.

Scoop hangs with a group of elite brothers who all own businesses and can have just about any woman in the city they chose. Our boss, John, is in the click, which is how we got invitations to come hang out at The Sugar Shack. The first night we showed up, all eyes were on us just like tonight.

Scoop had recently met us at the office so he treated us like queens. Sending drinks to our table and checking on us periodically during the night. I warned Macy that night that he was out of her league, but nawl, she had a thing for him and couldn't let it go. By the time we make it to the corner of her street, I turn to look at her.

"What happened, Macy?"

"Jo, he blew my mind. I have never experienced an orgasm like the one I had tonight, but in the end, that's all it was to him. Jo, how could I be so stupid?"

"Look, don't say that. Did you make him wear a condom?"

"He didn't put his thang in me, just his finger and tongue."

"Your behind should've come out of there happy as a peacock. What happened in between orgasms to Jo let's go?"

"Scoop asked me what I wanted and when I finally told him I wanted him, he fed me some crap about I ain't ready for what I'm asking for. You get me off, and then turn me off in the same setting. I feel like he's played me like a cheap whoremonger."

I touch my girl on the arm. "He knows you're not that, Macy. From what P-baby told me, Scoop has been checking for you just as long as you've been checking for him. Whatever happened between the two of you is something both of you wanted. It was consensual because you didn't scream, and memorable because you got fulfilled."

She smiles. "It was good, but Jo, I want more. It's been six years since I've been with a man and I prayed that if I ever had an intimate relationship with another man, it would be him. But I'm too old for this quick hit ish. Maybe, if he would have caught me six years ago, I'd play the game how he wants to, but that girl ain't me and I'm not her anymore."

"I feel you friend, but huh." I hand her five one hundred dollar bills I pull from my bra.

"What the...no, who and what did you do?"

I laugh. "Girl, I'm going to leave you with that pain. I said I ain't sleeping with nobody unless it's my husband, but I dang shole came close tonight. You coming from back there like you did was all the escape I needed." We both laugh. "I just happened to get what he called a down payment."

"Well, you always said, 'God will provide an escape for you.' My problem is I just never take Him up on His escape."

"Exactly, and that's why you are right here in this car with me now, feeling all that pain that comes from pleasure. When will you ever learn?"

"I guess Betty Wright played on Momma's record player a little too long, because this chick is still singing, 'No Pain, No Gain.'"

"That part. Now go in the house, wash your nasty behind, and get ready to deal with whatever. I love you and I'll call you tomorrow."

I give Macy the keys to her car and sit in my car until she goes into the house. She blinks the light two times, which signals she's in and the alarm is set. I pull off, shaking my head.

Man, I just dodged a bullet.

CHAPTER 7
SOMETHING AIN'T RIGHT
SCOOP

"Calm down old boy...maybe next time," I tell my manhood as I'm left standing in my office wondering what just happened. One minute Macy is basking in juices and swirling on my tongue, and the next she's trying to get out of my office as quickly as she can.

Women...who knows what they're ever thinking?

I go to my bathroom to adjust my boy, wash my face, and brush my teeth. Right now, I should be making her cum again and watching her eyes sparkle with pure delight.

What just happened? I ask myself again.

"Scoop, get your shit together, you're still at work, dude." I don't know if it's the fact that I've been holding out or that Macy tasted so good, but all I can think about is what I want to do to her next.

I look at myself one last time and then I make my way back to the bar area in my spot.

"Negro, what did you do? One minute I'm begging for some sweet stuff and the next, my girl exiting stage left behind some shit you did."

"Hold on, P," because I refuse to call a grown man a baby. I finish stacking the drink shelf and toss some almost empty bottles in the trash. "Meet me in my office?"

I click my key fob to unlock my office door. One thing is...I trust Philip with my life. We've been boys since the sixth grade and he knows me like a book. Maybe he can help me sort this junk out with Macy. I finish up and then go to my office where I find Philip sitting at my desk.

"Well, I know what you didn't do because I don't smell crap in here but that black berry candle."

"F' you, but man she belted on me."

"No shit, and whatever you did blocked my boy from my dream ride. What the heck did you say, because I know you said something stupid?"

"Man, the first thing I did was ask her what she wanted. I was hoping she said she wanted me. Dude, you know how long I've been scoping her out. Then to get her in here for the first time and I ask her what she wants and all she wants is for me to screw her. Man, that disappointed your boy."

"Well, did you screw her?"

I roll my eyes because now he is just being nosey. "Technically, no."

P looks at me like I've lost my mind. "Okay, so let's get this straight. You've been feening for this woman a whole year. You get her in your office for the first time. She tells you she wants you to screw her. And your dumb ass let her walk. Something ain't right with this."

I stare at the wall where I had Macy pinned. "It threw me off, man. I guess I expected more than she's willing to give. Then when she comes back on the backend and says she wants me, then I was tripping...me or my boy?"

"Negro, your boy is a part of you. How the hell are you gonna separate your boy from the man? So, when she said that, what did your dumb ass say then?"

"I actually said, 'I don't think you're ready for what you're asking for.'"

"Now I see why she stormed out of here. The woman enjoys you, then says she wants you after you've pleased her, in whatever way that was, and you tell her she's not ready. So to a woman, you took her there and basically said she didn't deserve what you made her feel. You gotta fix this because if you don't, I'll never get that fine ass Josephine on top of my boy."

"If your game was tight, you could." I laugh.

He's looking at me all crazy and strange so I ask him, "What, P?"

"I was just thinking, you in here f'ing up and I was out there doing the same thing. Josephine wanted to check on Macy and I told her she's probably doing what we should be doing. How insensitive was that? Man, I wish having money came with a tutorial on how to talk to women."

"What the hell does money have to do with any of this?" I ask Philip, and I watch this stupid look appear on his face. It's the look he's had whenever he's been acting like a prideful prick.

"I gave Josephine a grand as a downpayment."

"A downpayment? So basically, you treated her like a thot and pimped her at the same time."

"Dude, it wasn't like that. She told me this story about her daddy saying a man puts his money where he wants his boy to be. Shiitttt, I was just making sure there were no questions in her mind as to where I want my boy."

"Now who's the dummy? A pocket down by a thousand dollar dummy. Boy, get your ass out of here so I can count my money and go home." I shake my head because Philip just a giver by nature and no matter what opportunity he's presented with to give, good or bad, he's always the one shelling out money.

"You're leaving early tonight, huh?"

"Dude, I can't work like this. Macy f'd me up in all kinds of ways in my head. Now, I have to figure out how to fix this."

Philip stands up just as my DJ starts playing, "Feenin" by Jodeci and he bursts out laughing.

"That's your jam right there, ain't it, you feenin butthole."

I look at Philip because whether he knows it or not, I'm definitely that at this point. I either gotta get this girl, or get her off my mind.

Philips smiles. "You gotta stop playing on old girl's top and go on and tell her you've been wanting her just as long as she's been coming into The Sugar Shack. Nawl, I take that back. You've been feenin ever since the day you walked into John's office and saw her at that front desk."

"Dude, bye."

How am I going to fix this crap?

CHAPTER 8
THE OLD WAY WON'T WORK
MACY J

I toss and turn all night, thinking about what happened at The Sugar Shack. I finally get a chance to be in the arms of the man I've been dreaming and drooling over for a year, and he tells me I'm not ready.

One mind wanted to say, "Oh, I was ready for your finger and tongue to be all in my cat, but I'm too broke, busted, and plain to be on your arm."

Yet again, I said nothing.

I just walked out like a pouting child and left. Another missed opportunity to tell a man how I feel because I clammed up.

I start kicking my legs and throwing my arms like I'm fighting with my bed and the truth is, that's how I want to fight myself; the part of me who lets people do or say whatever they want to me and I say nothing. The part that's always second-guessing my responses instead of just putting them on the table.

Then, to think that trifling negro sucked me crazy and I walked out in a headspace hangover. That's more than enough reason to never go back there again.

I look over at the clock.

It's only four-thirty. Thirty minutes more than it was the last time I looked over at the huge, red, glaring numbers. I can't win without losing. Every time I fall asleep, I go right back to The Sugar Shack. When I open my eyes, I still see Scoop. *Macy, carry your behind to sleep.*

I pull the covers over my head and close my eyes once again.

The ringing of the phone wakes me up.

"Lord, please let it be late morning," I say before I pick up my phone.

"Good morning."

"Get your ass up. I went to The Sugar Shack with you last night, and you need to go to church with me this morning."

I beg, "Jo, please don't make me go today."

"Lie, now get up and I'll be there in the next hour."

I hang up the phone and realize I've just missed another opportunity to say what I want to say. She likes playing these saint verses sinners games and I don't. If I'm a sinner, let Jesus's grace do what He wants it to, and let me navigate through life how I feel is best for me. Somehow, Josephine doesn't understand that.

She tells me over and over that His grace doesn't work where there is no faith.

I hear her but right now, who wants to talk faith after begging to be screwed? See, my point exactly. Either I'm real or I'm fake and I can't fake with a God who knows everything.

I get out of bed, because even in all of that, I know our pact. If she goes to the club with me, I go to church with her. I'm just glad her pastor is an old man so while he is speaking, the only thing I'm worried about is him falling.

Now, if she were a member of that Turner guy's church...I'd have a whole set of different problems. The dude looks like he could be Scoop's brother and he's got those same funky gray eyes.

I pull out a pink flowered dress, with a matching pink summer hat, and my open toe pink shoes with the green flower on the ankle strap. Now, somebody needs to water me down because my vjay is still hot from last night.

Dang, I don't feel like this. But somehow I've discovered whenever I don't want to go to church, there will always be something there for me. I move through the house and by the time Jo honks, I'm dressed and ready to get this adventure over.

I'm listening intently to the pastor who says, "It's easy to get into sin, but it's hard to get out of it. Sin is like having the end of a rope and the opposition–which is the sin you like– is slowly but with steady preciseness trying to pull you into the pond."

Man, that's just what happened to me last night. I've been without sex for six whole years, and that sucker put me on the rope and pulled my ass all the way in the pond. Excuse me, Lord, for cursing in Your house.

The pastor continues, "You have to learn how to build a resounding resolve. Tell the devil 'No.' If he talks to you, be bold enough to talk back to him. The only way he wins is if you let him."

He won't be winning here, because this vjay closed again. If he wants me, he's going to have to get me the right way. But Lord, that man put a tongue demon on me. I couldn't sleep or rest. I shake my head to come out of my thoughts then I focus as the pastor begins to make his invitation.

"If you are fighting against something that seems too strong for you to handle by yourself, invite the Lord to help you. Listen, the Lord wants to see you through this. He knows the struggles you face in life, but He also knows that you can do all things through Him. Let the Lord help you."

I get up from my seat and join the line of other parishioners who have confessed that they need the Lord.

The reason I swore off men was because I was tired of being a wet bar handing free squeezes, but at the end of the month struggling to make sure I had my house, car, and insurance money in the bank for the first. Had it not been for Josephine, I would have been just another wet bar last night.

I lift my hand when it's my turn. I hear the pastor, but my mind is saying, Thank You, Lord, for that five hundred dollars. That's my car note and some of my insurance money.

The pastor says, "Daughter, did you hear me?"

I lean in. "Pastor, please say it again."

He repeats himself. "God has a plan for you and He's going to give you the desire of your heart. You just can't use the old tricks to get new blessings. You need to simply wait on the Lord."

I nod my head. He said it in his language but I heard it in mine... B, you can't use your vjay to get a husband. Get the husband and then use the vjay to keep him. Lord, please forgive me, once again.

Dang it's hard navigating through life with men, tongues, fingers, and fantasies.

CHAPTER 9

NO MORE WILLING WORKERS
JOSEPHINE

It didn't take long for me to see that Macy really needed to be in service today. My girl took a hit last night, but the truth is...so did I. P-baby was saying all the right stuff, sharing, joking, and almost had me caving at the end of the rope.

My eyes immediately glance over a couple of rows over at Grady. He's everything any woman would want in a man, but the truth is, he's just not for me. Yes, it's taken me this long to finally admit my truth. Confession brings about cleansing, so today I'm making my own confession. *I don't want Grady.*

There's always a willing worker in the bunch, but the worker doesn't always meet the criteria. You use them because they're willing, despite them not being qualified. In our case, he's trying to make me happy, and I willingly let him. *Poor Grady.* I'm going to stop playing with Grady's heart. After last night, I realize I'm just not the girl to settle with the willing worker.

Macy and I get in my car after I've spoken to all the church mothers and greeted my people. She's been ready to go, but just like I waited on her last night, today is her turn. I look over at her and ask, "So how do you feel?"

She shrugs her shoulders. "Uhmm, sad."

"Okay," I answered, waiting for her to elaborate, and she does.

"I was really hoping for something special between Scoop and I, and now, the girl who makes all the wrong moves is now waddling in the despair of her choice."

I sympathize with her greatly, because none of us are perfect and every time I think I've gotten myself set to do something different, I fall back into the same rut. I nod and then ask, "When you went to that altar today, I was thinking about my own life. Macy, I'm so sick and tired of being the church girl, settling with a man I don't want, because he's all I felt I deserve or could get. I promise I feel unqualified in every area of my life, but something happened last night."

Macy looks at me wide-eyed. "What?"

I grin thinking about the moment. "When Philip gave me his full name, driver's license number, address, and all his personal information, I thought...this man must think something great about me. You know, I'd never give a stranger my information like that."

"Me either, I guess, but what's the difference between giving a man my personal information or my vjay? Heck, my vjay is more personal than all that crap."

I snicker. "Now you are definitely right about that." We both ponder over the statement.

"Jo, do you care about Grady?"

I shrug my shoulders. "I care, but not enough to share my entire life with him. Like, he's good enough to satisfy my urges, but not my heart. So, to be honest, I go through the motions of a woman in love, but afterwards, I have the baggage of a woman who did something she really didn't like." *Using people just isn't easy when you know Christ.*

Macy shakes her head. "I wish that was my lot. I gave myself to a man to do whatever he wanted, but at the end of the day, I still didn't get what I wanted."

I look over at my girl and see tears running down her face. I ask, "Macy, what did you want?"

She gave a light smile. "I wanted a gift for my gift. I went in there with no intentions, but every time I've ever stepped foot in The Sugar Shack, I hoped that Scoop would give me his heart. So there you have it, my truth. Can you imagine my shame? He drives me wild. I'm back there talking out of my head. Then after its over, I ask for him and he says, 'I'm not ready.' I just don't understand why he feels like that."

I pull over in the parking lot of one of our locally owned black restaurants, LaShelle's, turn off the engine, and turn slightly to look at Macy. "So let's go back to the beginning. When you went to the back..." I stretch out my hand so she can continue.

"He clicked the button to unlock the door to his office so I can use his bathroom. Even told me I never have to use the public restroom. I should've known that was b-s because I've been coming there for a full year and he's never offered his office or restroom to me. But I was too blind to see the set up."

I smile and nod. "That crap is so plain now."

"Yes, even a fool can see it, but I didn't last night. The first thing he asks me is, 'What did I want?' If I wasn't so hung up on my lack, I would have told him what I've practiced the entire year, 'Scoop, I want you.' Nawl, I had a six year deprived vjay, thumping and getting wet, and she controlled everything."

I laugh so hard. Not because I'm making fun of my girl but because I've been there before. In a place where my emotions overpower my intelligence. "So, friend, where do you go from here? Do you hang your head in shame or do you find a way to get the moment back?"

"That's a question I have yet to ask myself. I would think I'd rather hide in shame, but of course I know that's not the answer. To be honest, just because what happened did, doesn't mean I don't want him in my life. I need to figure this thing out and pinpoint how my life is going to intersect with love."

We clap hands. "Now that's one for the record books. I needed to just confess and today, I believe I started that journey. I know I don't want Grady and while he's trying to impress me, he could be living his best life, in love, and with a woman who loves him. So, the first step for me is to move out of Grady's way."

Macy laughs so hard. "I always told you to leave the willing work and find the man who makes you work."

I join in the laughter. "You did that. Transparent moment?"

"Transparent moment," Macy yells. It's a thing we do when we're about to expose some deep thoughts.

"I felt like having a willing worker was better than not having one at all. But look where that got me. Right next to my vjay sharing best friend with no man."

"Oh, you are wrong for that but just like the pastor said, 'God's going to give me just what I want.' I don't know when, who, or how, but I'm working on doing something different in my life until love finds me."

We clap hands, because that sounds good to me. "Let's go eat."

"I'm right behind you."

No more willing workers.

CHAPTER 10
GIRL CAN'T TALK
MACY J

The hectic Monday morning work day is taking a toll on Jo and I. Our boss, John, knows that Mondays are the worst day of the week for us because his clients start ringing the phones at eight thirty in the morning. Most of them are angry or disgruntled because of a weekend wreck or an after hour cancellation. But yet, he still has too many scheduled appointments and Zoom meetings which require us to lend him a helping hand.

One part of me wishes I could just pick up my purse and go home. He knows just like I do that my commitment to keeping the home I purchased is the noose that keeps me here. I look up at Josephine, who is just as frustrated as me. The fact that she still lives at home with her parents gives her another type of freedom.

I can't tell you how many times she cursed John flat out and walked out the door, only to have him begging her to come back before noon. *I can't take that chance.* And believe me, he knows it. That's why he puts me through hell sometimes and I just take his shit.

He wants to keep us close because we both know his business like the back of our hands. We treat his customers with respect, and we always dress professional and to perfection. So much so, his mother calls us John's Angels. We know if it had not been for the Lord, we would've kicked his ass, slashed his tires, and stole all his money. Her calling us angels reminds me that she's trusting us to take care of her no good son.

I look over at Josephine because it's almost time for lunch.

We have to be on top of stuff in this office because he will try to play us out of our break if we let him.

John used to try to make one of us go to lunch and the other stay, but we weren't having it. He soon found out it was our way or no way at all. So at eleven forty-five, the entire office shuts down for thirty-five minutes. Long enough for us to swallow our food, get a good gossip session, and a rest from that damn constantly ringing phone.

I walk the last customer to the door at eleven forty-two, and turn the 'Out For Lunch' sign around.

Josephine laughs. "Girl, these people have kicked our butts this morning."

"I know, right? I've been so busy I haven't had time to think about anything going on in my shabby life." We laugh.

Jo walks over to my desk. "Are you still getting those strange calls?"

I nod. "Yeah, but I just turned my phone off last night." I looked up at the door. "Josephine, don't turn around now, but Philip is walking toward the door."

"For real? Macy, stop lying."

"If I'm lying I'm dying, and I'm breathing just fine."

Her eyes get big. "Macy! How do I look? What the heck is he doing here?"

I giggle. "Your straight and cute, I might add. I don't have a clue. Probably to get you." I throw my hand at her and she laughs. "He even has a big bag in his hand. Let me put this dry sandwich in the trash."

"Really, Macy?" We laugh.

John comes from his office on the other side to open the door. I figure he must've seen Philip walking up. He opens the door. "What's up man?"

"Hey, John, I need to see Josephine." He comes inside holding on to the bag.

John points. "There she is over at her desk but please lock that door, man, because they're on lunch break."

Philip locks the door and then walks over to Josephine's desk.

"Hey, sweet lady, I got some more money to put where I want to be." He hands her an envelope and the bag.

I've never seen Josephine look so surprised. Then she starts talking loud enough for me to hear. "Listen, I don't need your money because I'm not a whore and you're not my pimp. Why are you here, P-baby?"

He never says one word but pulls Josephine in his arm and kisses her like a man who's been waiting forever to kiss the woman he loves. I'm sitting back watching the show play out in real time. I'm also cracking up because she looks like a duck caught in wire.

I get real quiet when P-baby says, "I don't need a whore and I'm not a pimp. I told you I've been praying that God would send me a wife, and you have six months to make up your mind if you want to be kept and protected."

I start swinging my arms in the air and kicking my legs. Bro-man putting that smack down. I'm also shaking my head because Josephine still hasn't said one word.

After he hugs her and kisses her cheek, he turns to leave and looks back. "Oh, and that's food for you and Macy, and I'll be by to pick you up tomorrow so you need to be dressed and ready at seven. I've already told John, you'll be off Wednesday so he needs to make whatever accommodations he has to."

"You're not the boss of me, Philip." Josephine finally says something that makes Philip and me break out into laughter.

"This shit isn't funny, Macy."

"Yes, it is," I hollered across the room then I say, "Thanks for the food, Philip."

He nods, unlocks the door, and walks right back out.

I have never seen Josephine like this with a man and it's funnier than watching Kevin Hart do his best jokes. Girl can't even talk around this man so I know he's all in her head. Two minutes later and she's still over there looking like she's been struck by lightning.

All I want is whatever is in that bag.

I march right over to her desk, open the bag, grab the plate with my name on it, and march right back to my desk. I open the container and smell the barbecue that came from Barbecue Heaven, the best place in town. "Girl, girl, that's your husband, because if he's gonna be bringing us lunch like this, I'll take your ass to the courthouse to marry him."

"I can't stand you, Macy. Your ass is gonna sell me out for some food."

"I love you."

He shut her DOWN!

CHAPTER 11
SWEET LADY
JOSEPHINE

I stand patiently by the front door waiting on P-baby. One part of me wants to just say, 'I'm not going,' but another part wants to see if he is really the man for me. Enclosed in the envelope was two thousand dollars. Enough money for me to share with Macy and buy me a small designer tote bag to put a day's worth of clothing in.

I was told to pack light, but to make sure I have something nice to wear to dinner. Macy and I decided that I should borrow her black one arm out sequined dress that she purchased from *Fashion Nova*. We both agreed that it would be perfect for a night out. At work, she put my hair in pin curls that flowed into a messy bun. I just have to make sure not to mess it up before he comes.

I am cute if I have to say so myself. I FaceTime Macy to let her see me and she agrees. We chit chat for a little while and I end the call when P-baby pulls up.

At exactly six forty-five, Philip pulls up in my yard. I open the door and try to hurry before he gets out of the car. However, he insists on getting out and coming in to meet my parents. *That's all the ammunition Momma needs to call all her sisters and church buddies.*

By the time he finishes talking to my parents, I can tell they already love him. My daddy is calling him son, and my mother is grinning like Philip came to pick her up. *I pray he's not a serial killer because he has my whole family hoodwinked.*

When he finally decides it's time for us to go, it's already seven twenty. Momma is telling me to enjoy myself and I'm just amazed at my daddy holding on to that box of cigars Philip gave him like they're worth more than me.

He puts me in his car and then puts my bag in the trunk. The chivalry is all fine and dandy, but I still want to know where the hell he's taking me. Twenty minutes later, we pull into a circular driveway at his house. I know because I remembered the address.

I thought we were going to dinner or somewhere.

He opens the door and he can tell by the look on my face that I'm tripping. When I stand out of the car, he bends down, kisses me, and then asks, "Jo, do you trust me?"

I roll my eyes. "I must do. I'm dressed up and at your house. Anyway, you've gotten permission from everyone I love to have me. If that's not trust, I don't know what is."

P-baby starts laughing so loud. His laugh is warming my heart. He takes me by my hand and walks me toward his front door.

"Welcome home, my sweet lady."

I cut my eyes at him and blush. This Negro knows how to use his words and he still ain't getting none.

A lady greets us at the door. "Good evening, Lady Josephine. Would you like anything to drink?" she asks and I quickly say, "No thank you."

Philip leans down and whispers, "Rosa's been my housekeeper for ten years and her husband, Hosea, tends to the grounds."

That makes me feel a little better. But if I become his wife Rosa can stay at home and take care of her husband while I take care of mine.

"Right this way," Rosa says. I follow her with Philip walking behind me.

In the beautifully decorated dining area is a table for two, draped with the most expensive seven candle candelabra surrounded in red roses as the centerpiece. I would have sworn it was the bride and groom's table at a wedding. Philip pulls my chair out and after I sit down, he pushes my chair in the perfect position.

"Thank you," I say, smiling up at him.

As soon as he sits down, three men with instruments come from around the corner, playing Jacquees song "Get You." It's one of my favorite songs, and I can't believe it when a man comes from behind them singing the song to me.

Rosa brings out our food and as the miniature band is playing so many songs I love, we talk about just about everything. He really makes me laugh.

After dinner, the band is back to performing and the singer is singing a song by Tyrese, "Sweet Lady." At one point, I just put my hand over my face because no one has ever done anything this thoughtful for me. Philip takes my hand and sings a little of the song as well. *He really can sing.*

"Oh, so you have chops?" I laugh and he keeps singing. *About to sing me right out of my panties.*

Then I get up from my chair and start dancing. When the men in the band start looking at my butt, he sends them out, claps his hands, and music starts flowing through the speakers.

"Now, you can dance," Philip says as he picks up his drink. "But come right here." He points directly in front of him.

I don't know what it is, but dancing for him is turning me on just as much as it is exciting him. I pull my dress up and straddle his lap, performing the most provocative lap dance I've ever done for a man.

After a while, he says, "Stand up and let me see you, baby," as "Sexy" by Tank pours through the speakers. Midway through the song, Philip stands up, mashes a button and says, "My wife and I need to be alone."

I hear through the intercom, "Yes, sir, Mr. Micheals."

"Why didn't I get the memo?" I say as he pulls me to his body and starts kissing me like I already belong to him. *This man can kiss. Where the hell have you been?* "I'm married and don't even know it."

Then he pulls back. "Jo, stop playing with me."

Philip bends down and before I know it, he has me securely in his arms. He looks at me. "Do I have permission to love you tonight? Give me permission to take you places you've never gone and give you all of me, as you give me all of you."

"Wait," I demand and he stops walking. I touch his face. "Only if you plan on loving me for the rest of our lives."

Philip starts smiling and kisses me again but doesn't reply.

I pull out of the kiss. "I'm serious, Philip. I don't want to be fucked. I want to be loved for the rest of my life. If that's not your intention, you can take me home right now." *I ain't messing up like Macy did...your cock is secondary to commitment for me.*

He doesn't say one word but as if I already knew what's up, he carries me to his bedroom.

It's about to go to another level.

CHAPTER 12
CAUGHT SLIPPIN'
MACY J

I look over at my clock, it's almost seven o'clock. I know Josephine is about to go on her date. Just as I am about to pick up the phone to call her, she Facetimes me.

"Hey, chick. Oh my goodness, you are absolutely beautiful! Girl, you are going to mess poor P-baby's mind right on up tonight."

Josephine smiles. "Thanks to you and this pretty dress, I feel beautiful. And Macy, on the slick, Momma is acting like she's so happy I'm going out with someone new."

"We all are. We are sick of watching you settle with Grady but it wasn't our call to make. You are a grown woman and me and Momma decided to mind our business."

She grins. "But dang, y'all could have told me. Maybe I wouldn't have wasted so much time."

"Look, all things happen for a reason. Try to have fun. Give Philip your best effort because I really do believe he's the one for you."

Jo blushes. "Awe thanks, sissy. Well, he's pulling up now, I'll check on you tomorrow. Love you."

"You better and love you back." We disconnect the call.

My girl really does deserve to have a man who she can love as much as he loves her. I swear I'm not jealous, although I had to remind myself of this a couple times today. You always want your girl to be happy, but sometimes you wonder why it doesn't happen for you both at the same time.

I shouldn't have stormed out. I should have given him a chance to tell me what he meant. *It's too late now.* Then it hits me. *Maybe not.* I know it has to be Scoop blowing up my phone because I've never seen those numbers before ever. I'm not answering because I'm just not ready to cave in yet.

Josephine told me to just make sure I don't start playing childish games with him, but I'm not. He really hurt me, and I need him to understand that I don't have to experience pain to feel love. If there is one thing I know, the only way to show a man that you mean business is for you to act like you're done. A man will humble down if you ever make him feel like you're on the way out the door and mean it.

The problem with us women is we can't stay away too long. We will say, 'I'm leaving you,' and be back in a man's bed before the clock strikes twelve.

Not Macy J and not this time.

I want Scoop to come to me like I've been going to The Sugar Shack for the last year. I promised myself, and the Lord, that I am waiting to be found and I'm not taking anything less than. I also stopped lying to myself about sex. Had I not been trying to be so high and mighty about being celibate for six years, I wouldn't have fallen so easily.

Pride is a b all by itself, for real.

As soon as I felt like I had life licked, I fell. In the midst of my fall I realized that I'm just as hot and horny as the next female. Like the singer says, 'girls need love too.' I just don't understand why girls fake like we don't want a man's package just as much as men want ours.

After Saturday night with Scoop, I'm never acting like I'm

super-locked and I'm saying what I want. If I want to be screwed, then that's what I want. If I want my vjay licked until it feels raw, then that's what I want. If I want him to watch as I play with myself, then that's what I want. F' feeling guilty.

I flip through the television in hopes to find something worth watching. My mind is all over the place. Maybe I should just go to The Sugar Shack, go up to his ass, and kiss him as hard as he kissed me. *That's it. I'm going.*

I get up, put on my jeans, and a shirt. I pull my hair in a ponytail and put on my cap. I give my face a light beat, one last look over, grab my keys, and head out the door. The worst he can do is tell me to get out.

I drive to The Sugar Shack singing "Come Through" by H.E.R. I actually love all her music because she reminds me of my favorite artist of all times, Prince. *Yeah, I'm coming through tonight.* My mind is on nothing but making sure when I leave he knows I want a repeat.

I turn the corner and have to blink my eyes. Who's standing outside talking to a woman...Scoop. They must be having a really good conversation because he's laughing so hard and she's smiling too damn hard.

At first, I started to swing in the parking lot, put my lights on bright, and then act like a plumb fool. *But why? He's not my man because he said I'm not ready.* My darn heart feels like it's about to beat out of my chest.

"Man!" I scream. Then an explosion of tears rips from my heart and flows from my eyes. *I have messed around and lost him before I even had the chance to have him.*

I pick up my phone, then remember where Jo is, and I'll never be that selfish and mess up her night because mine is feeling like hell. I pull into the first parking lot I find because driving while crying is just as deadly as driving drunk, and cry until my tears fade, but my heart feels no better.

I use the Kleenex in my console to blow my nose. After I

take a couple of deep breaths to calm my soul, I thank the Lord. Why? I realize that time is of the essence. While I'm wasting time trying to make him feel some kind of way by not answering the phone, another woman is willing and ready to talk.

I push the start button right as "Damage" by H.E.R. flows through the speaker. This girl is definitely talking to me tonight. I wasn't careful and now...

This b done caught me slippin.

CHAPTER 13
SLOW
JOSEPHINE

The bedroom is just as beautiful as the dining area. Red roses all over the room and it is so thoughtful that it makes me cry. I've seen this on the television, but I never in a million years thought a man would do this for me.

"Look at all of this. Philip, is this all for me?"

He laughs and lays me on his huge bed.

"Josephine, who else is it for? And you best believe there's so much more in store for you. Now, give me permission to undress you."

I smile and that's all the permission he needs. He picks up my legs, one by one, kisses them, as he unbuckles the strap on my heels.

Damn, I'm glad I wore my red bottoms.

Once my shoes are off, he puts them on his dresser. Philip comes back to the bed and stands right in front of me. He undresses with me watching him take off every piece. When his cock comes out he asks, "Is this big enough for you, Jo?"

Hell, yeah! I would have said but I can't get anything out. My throat ain't cooperating with my mouth, because my mind is processing how hard and long his thang is.

He pulls me by my butt to the edge of the bed and then raises me up in a sitting position. "Touch it, Josephine, and see if it's as hard as you want it."

I look at him. I touch it. It's hard but I can't do this. Don't do it Jo. "Philip," I dang near whisper.

"Jo, I'm not going anywhere." As if he knows my thoughts, he continues, "Feel under that pillow." He points to the pillow right by my hand.

My eyes bulge, and he says, "Get it."

I pull from under the pillow a ring bigger than any ring I've ever seen before. On Instagram yeah, but in person...I don't have anyone in my circle with the kind of money to afford a ring like this.

Philip takes it from my hand and asks, "Will you be my wife?"

This man is proposing while his cock sticking straight toward my lips. I want to suck it. Focus Josephine...answer the question.

"Look at me." He lifts my head with his hands and I obey him by looking into his eyes.

I guess he couldn't resist because he bends down and licks my lips. Then he asks me again, "Will you marry me?"

Talk b. Talk. "Philip, are you sure it's me that you want? You don't even know me." I've seen him at The Sugar Shack more than once, but the other night was our first time ever holding conversations. *Surely that wouldn't constitute us knowing one another.*

"You think, huh?" He smiles. "You are Josephine Jackson, the daughter of Nette and Joseph Jackson. You live at 3526 Blom Street. You work as an insurance agent, and you love the Lord with all of your heart. I know this because no matter how late you stay at the club on Saturday, Sunday always finds you in God's house. Now, if I don't know you, who does?"

Who is this man, why does he know me, and how the heck did I get so blessed? Finally I say, "But Philip, you don't think we're rushing this?"

He kisses me. "Little lady, I'm grown. I know when I'm looking at a piece of me. You don't think today is my first time meeting your parents, do you?"

I look at him with bulging eyes. "Huh?"

"Baby, I've had lunch with your parents twice since Saturday and have asked them for your hand in marriage. I've even spoken with Macy a time or two in the last few days. Jo, I know who you are. I just need you to know it."

I'm so emotional right now. The fact that he's already included my parents and my girl. The fact that he's so sure about me. *Damn, this shit feels like an arranged marriage, but I want it.* "Yes, Philip, I'll marry you."

He puts the rock on my finger, then he kisses me with passion and I think I'm falling in love. Then with ease and perfection, he pulls my dress over my head, and unfastens my bra. With my girls in full display, Philip kisses and caresses my nipples. I watch him as he takes ownership of my body.

"Josephine," he calls my name with the sweetest sensitivity I've ever known.

I answer, "Yes."

He towers over me but bends to kiss me, and then he says, "I believe in having a wedding, but I don't believe we have to have one to be married. Tonight, when I claim you in every way a man can claim a woman, you will be my wife. Plan whatever you want, whenever you want, but know, after tonight, we are already married in the sight of God and in our hearts and minds."

Tears start to flow from my eyes. Philip kisses my eyes and then my lips again. When he has dried each tear with his lips, he stands up straight, pulls my legs up, plants kisses on my toes and feet, not missing any spots. By the time he makes it to my thighs, I'm going crazy. I want to beg him to just give it to me, but I enjoy him as he takes his time enjoying me.

The music has been playing softly in the background, but before now, I wasn't paying much attention. Now, I'm listening as Robin Thicke tickles my ears, and feeling as Philip Micheals tickles my body.

Philip parts my vjay with his fingers. "Sex Therapy" is flowing as I close my eyes. He gently runs his finger from my clit to the opening of my vjay and plays there for a moment until it is wet and making popping sounds. Then Philip plants kisses on my heated spot and flicks my clit with his tongue and it's driving me wild. Just when he has me on edge, and I'm pushing my body up to meet his tongue, he stands up and strokes his cock as I watch.

He pulls in sync with Jamie Foxx's song "Slow." *His fucking playlist sounds familiar and it's as fire as this moment.* He's pulling his package nice and slow and when I see his head release juices, I sit up because I just want to taste him.

I lick him, and then pull it into my mouth. *He tastes so good.*

"Do you want this, Josephine? Tell me you want this."

I pull him from my mouth but lick him. Then I finally say, "I want all of this, Philip. Every part of you."

He bends, wraps his arms around my legs, and pulls me to the edge of his bed. He teases me with the tip of his cock. Taking it in and out until I begin to beg for him. "I want you, Philip. I want you now."

"I'm yours and every piece of this is yours," he says as he teases me until I'm boiling over with desire. When I've begged enough, he finally puts it all the way in. Slow and steady. Inch by inch.

It feels so good! He's big but cautiously sensitive so it doesn't hurt. I moan. I groan.

Philips looks at me as he talks to me. "Take it in, baby. Pull it all in. Grip me, Jo. Yes, baby."

I swirl on him faster, using my muscles to clap it with every pull, and then he says, "I'm about to nut baby."

I cry, "Give it to me, Philip." He shakes and I scream. At the same time, we explode on each other.

Philips pulls out of me and then he bends down to claim my juices with his mouth. I feel myself about to explode again. *This has never happened to me...two orgasms back to back.* Nice and slow, he licks then he touches, then he grips, and I watch as his cock inflates as if it never went down.

Get ready, b, it's about to be a long night.

CHAPTER 14
ALL THE JUICE
MACY J & JOSEPHINE

I walk around the office, filling up the shelves with all the necessary tools for a successful day at work. I'm an hour early and patiently waiting for Josephine. I texted her last night to come an hour early so she can give me all the juice. As normal, she's late but I smile when she appears and walks toward the building.

My girl is walking with a new twist. Philip must've rocked her boat. I laugh.

"Good morning," she says as she walks in. I heard her but that's not what I'm waiting for.

"Whatever, let me see it!"

Josephine holds her hand out in front of me and my eyeballs almost pops out of their sockets. "What the...! Baby, that's an engagement, wedding, dinner, graduation, and congratulations ring. Brother paid a grip for that thing."

Josephine giggles. "I know, right?" We make our 'we so happy' noise and start hugging and jumping around like two school aged girls. "Macy, he's everything I've ever wanted in a man. I keep asking God, have I been this faithful?"

"Technically, you have if it constitutes how much you stay

at that church." I roll my eyes. "But if faith and being faithful is what it takes to get a man and rock like that, I'll be on the row next to you from now on." We both laugh.

"He's everything, Macy. Gentle, thoughtful, kind, and I know exactly how Ruth felt to be gleaning in Boaz's field and to have his attention. Girl, it's wonderful."

I smile because I can see the glow all over my friend. "You'll be pregnant by next month because the way you are glowing, I know it's love."

"Girl! I keep telling myself, 'you can't love him this fast,' but my heart is speaking a different language. Macy, I can't get enough of him and I'm all in. Whether it leads to blissful happiness or fighting to be free, I'm in for every part of this ride."

"Well, shit's been going crazy for me. I pulled up on Scoop the other night and he is outside talking to a woman. When I tell you that thing broke me into pieces."

Josephine put her purse and bags down and came back to my desk. "Say that one more time."

"I went to The Sugar Shack, and when I got there, Scoop was outside talking to a woman. He was laughing and she was giggling, and all I could do was drive to the store on the corner, sit in their parking lot, and cry. I guess I waited too long."

Josephine hugs me. "But no, Macy, that can't be right. P-baby just told me yesterday that Scoop's been in love with you. He didn't approach you because the lying ass boss of ours had him thinking he was checking for you."

"What!"

Josephine puckers her lips. "That part."

"Wow! I promise I kept thinking he must be a homosexual, because no matter how much I flirted, he never took the bait."

Josephine laughs. "Now you know why."

"That dirty sucker. But that still doesn't explain why he'd have another woman in his face."

"Uh huh, but you have been dodging his calls, Macy. Philip

said that Scoop has called you a thousand times and you won't pick up the phone. Girl, stop blocking your blessing."

I roll my eyes. "Says the woman who just decided to embrace hers."

"That's right and all I'm saying to you is that I don't want you to miss out on this feeling. Macy, both Philip and Scoop are good guys and if you allow that man to get away, it won't be anyone's fault but yours."

"That's what made me get up and go by there, and what had me sitting up in Bible study last night without you. Pastor taught about life being so much easier when you learn how to love. In all of my years, I never realized how important it is for us to love, show love, and be loved."

Josephine has her hand over her mouth. "I know you are in love if you go to church twice in one week. Jesus, Lord God, don't ever let her fall out of love again. It's a miracle!" She throws up her arms like a tele-evangelist and laughs.

"Whatever, Josephine, I do realize where I went wrong and I know I should have given him a chance to communicate and myself as well." I nod. "I listened in Bible study without cursing too, because it was like God is helping me with my mistake right through the mouth of the pastor. And I made a commitment to learn my own love language and how to communicate what I felt. Just in case I ever had the opportunity to be with Scoop again."

Josephine smiles and touches my arm. "Believe me, sissy, you will. From what P-baby says, you two are meant for each other. And you know best friends know this information. By the way, thanks for giving Philip the songs off my playlist that I love. The boy was playing too many of my jams for me not to know I'd been set up. But they shole did sound good."

I fall over in my chair laughing. "Busted."

"You damn right you busted, and had me busting it wide open to Jamie Foxx singing, "Slow." Baby, and when Robin

Thicke's "Sex Therapy" started playing, I said that heifer done set me up. We had it going on up in that house and he already wants me to move all my things to his house."

I buck my eyes as I look at Jo. I knew he was serious, but the ring and him wanting her to move. *This is real.* "What are you going to do?"

"Friend, I'm packing boxes today and by the way, we have exactly eight weeks to plan my wedding."

"Well, darn, Josephine, y'all ain't playin no games, are you? But you better believe I'll be an arch ordering, tablecloths finding, napkin folding, and flower arranging nut."

"I know and that's why I'm not paying anyone but you to make my day special. Thank you for dragging me to The Sugar Shack, sissy. I owe you everything."

"No, ma'am, you don't owe me a thing. That's what sisters do for one another; they push each other into crap just to satisfy the other and sometimes it works in their favor."

"Amen."

Lord, I'm leaving this in Your hands.

CHAPTER 15

A BETTER ANSWER

SCOOP

Every time that door opens, I'm looking at it like she's about to walk in. Thursday night ladies drink for free–but no Macy. I can't get this girl off my mind.

I'm fucking her in my dreams. Tasting her in my mouth. Even calling her around the clock but she's not answering any of my calls. I'm not the one to be denied. Then again, I can see if I fucked up, but that's not the case here.

She stormed her ass out of The Sugar Shack like I played her. I didn't. All I know is when I give a woman the right to say we are together, we are together. I keep replaying that night in my mind; which isn't helping me one bit. But every time I do, the only thing I can see her pulling away from is me. *Is P right? Did me saying she wasn't ready hurt her?*

Shit, Macy. "Answer the phone and at least tell me what I did wrong," I whisper.

"You said something, boss?" my DJ asked.

"Nawl, Tamika, I'm good." I see her eyebrows furrow and her lips pucker. That's her 'that's bullshit' look.

"I've been watching you and no you're not good. Why don't you go get her?"

I don't share my business with my employees, but Tamika is like my sister. Judging by the way she's looking at me, I ain't going to feed her no crap. "I would if I knew where she lived. I was trying to respect the game so I had to stay as far away as I could and learn as little information as possible."

"Give me a few." Tamika picks up her phone and walks away from the counter.

"What's up?" I greet a couple fellows who I'm connected with through our business association. We've been meeting at my spot for ten years now to connect, support one another, and give leads if there's any to be given.

Oh, there's John. I move from behind my counter over to the space where we meet. "John, let me holla at you."

John and I have known one another since the sixth grade as well. "Look, has Macy been at work?"

He squints his eyes through his glasses. "Why the sudden interest in Macy?"

"Man, who the hell you think you are questioning. Just answer my question." I'm pissed enough to punch him because this low down trifling MF had me thinking Macy was cutting for him.

John grins. He, like all the other guys, knows when I'm mad, I'm mad. They all know not to mess with me and it's not because I'm a bully. I'm just a good dude but I've learned if you let folks shit on you, they will. I don't do stupidity and disloyalty.

"Yeah, she's been there. I'm about ready to fire her because I want a secretary who is willing to give me something in return."

I look at him. Choose your mother-fucking words kindly dude. "Give you what?"

"You know," and before John can say another word, I have my hand around his neck and his back pinned against my glass. I whisper, "John, if you fire Macy or Jo, lay a hand on either of them, say something stupid, or breathe the wrong way toward them, your Momma will be picking your casket color. Do you understand?"

John tries to speak but I have his throat.

"Let him go, Scoop. Come on, man, don't do this in your place," Philip pleads. "John is our boy. The negro just talk too much."

I release John while he's gasping for air. I bend down beside him on the floor. "Macy is off limits and if she ever tells me you broke our code, I'll break your neck."

John shakes his head.

I've never had a problem turning into a monster on a man. Especially one who acts like he's not going to respect a female, and we all know John has the tendencies to try to act all hard.

After the commotion dies down, I go back to the bar to calm my racing mind. I wasn't feeling much like conversing and I sure didn't feel like dapping up anybody. *They can miss me at that meeting tonight and have it without me.*

Tamika puts "Let's Chill" by Guy on. After she sets a rotation of records, she comes over to where I am standing and places her hand lightly on my shoulder. "Here you go, boss." She hands over a piece of paper. "Listen, we've got The Sugar Shack tonight. Why don't you take care of this and I'll call you if anything goes wrong."

Ordinarily, I never leave my spot. One, I have too many responsibilities and two, I have women working and I never want them in my spot unprotected. I have body guards working around the clock, but I'm my first choice for serving and protecting. But just like Tamika knows, I know. I have entirely too much on my mind and that's when Negros will catch you slippin. *Like John.*

"Say, Philip," I shout out over the club and beckon for him when he turns around. "Man, I need to go handle some business. Can you hang out here until Tamika closes the doors tonight?"

"You ain't said nothing but a thang. You handle your business, bro, and please get that damn girl so you can chill out. You dune scared the hell out of poor John. Boxers are probably tracked with all kinds of shit stains." Philip laughs and though it's funny, I don't have the energy for jokes.

"I'll call him and apologize tomorrow. He just rubbed me the wrong way at the right time. Man, this girl is turning me into a monster and if I don't go do something about the way things are between us, I'm gonna lose it."

"You already did that. The way you just went off on John was something else. So yes, you need to go do just that and if by chance she's with Josephine, tell her I'm looking for her and I'll see her when I get home."

"You staying with her parents too?"

"Hell nawl, Negro. She's moving boxes to our home today. Ya boy told you I ain't gettin no younger and I'm f'ing with Josephine for the rest of our lives." We laugh then dap one another up.

"I got you, dude. And Philip, man, say a prayer for me."

"I got you, man. Go get your woman and when you get her, please don't let her go."

"Man we both know you can't keep no one who doesn't want to be kept. I'm going to ask her the same question and hopefully this time, she'll give me a better answer."

Because I want her.

CHAPTER 16
A SWEET SURPRISE
MACY J

I walk through the doors of my home and straight to the bathroom.

All I need right now is a bubble bath, some lavender Epsom salt, and the sounds of the late Aaliyah. I call out, "Alexa, play Aaliyah radio station on Pandora." When I'm tired or missing my momma, her music is my go to, and today I'm both. As the music starts, I move around to the beat, gathering my necessities for the perfect bath.

My mind starts thinking about how hectic the work day was. Josephine missed one day and it has us so far behind, we worked like slaves to catch up. I want to cry but say, "If I'm going to continue to work for John, I have to become a licensed agent." I cringe at the thought even now, because that's not my passion.

I've been thinking a lot about my future and my dream job. That would definitely be starting a record label and signing artists who the world has overlooked. I love music. I love everything it represents. From the time I could talk, I could sing, and I have to give my mother the credit for that. She was a music girl herself and no matter how depressed she was, she always used music to show me her love.

I miss my momma. Sometimes more than at other times, but either way she's such a huge missing piece. I appreciate Josephine's mother for moving right into the mother's role, but no one can replace your mother.

I hang my robe, pull off my clothes, and step into the tub.

As soon as my head hits the tub pillow, my mind goes straight to Scoop. I shake my head trying to shake him out of my mind. The last thing I want is to be so wrapped up in him and us that I miss sharing in Josephine's happiness.

Shake back, Macy J, coveting isn't your lot.

I am only relaxing for about ten minutes when I hear a sound.

I open my eyes because it sounds like my door ringer is chiming. *It is. Now who could this be?* I stand up, step out of the tub, dry off a little so I won't track water, and then I put on my white robe.

"Just a minute," I yell. "Who is it?" I ask with my hand stretched out to reach the doorknob.

"It's Mark." He's my neighbor who feels like a little brother. For anyone else, I would have run and put on clothes. He's family and I feel safe being in a robe around him. However, I pull my belt tight and make sure I'm fully covered.

I smile as I open the door. "Hey, bro, what's going on?"

"I was just trying to make sure all your trash has been taken out. You know tomorrow's trash day."

I nod. "Yes, and I promise I have two bags in the kitchen and one out back. Come on in."

I see a white car that looks like Scoop's driving really slow but yet, I close the door because he doesn't know where I live.

I'm shocked when I open the door to let Mark out. Scoop is walking toward us and his facial expression is denoting anger.

Then with a harsh tone he says, "Oh, so this why you haven't been answering my calls, Macy. It's like this now."

I don't answer him but instead I thank Mark for coming to get my trash.

Mark smiles. "You're welcomed, Macy, anytime."

I smile and say, "Tell your wife that I love her and definitely thank her for sharing her husband with me." And then look directly in Scoop's eyes with my lips puckered.

Mark blushes. "You're the only family we have. See you later." Then he looks at Scoop. "Mark." He holds out his fist.

"Scoop."

"Nice to meet you, man."

"You too," Scoop says.

I ask as I snicker, "Want to come in?" *What a sweet surprise?* Then I move as he steps over the threshold of my door. I sure hope my ring recorded his facial expression when he saw Mark coming out of my house. If you ask me, he looked like a man on the verge of catching his wife cheating.

I explain my attire. "I was actually in the tub when Mark knocked on my door. Do you mind letting me finish?"

"Only if I can watch," Scoop says as he grabs my hand and pulls me to him.

I shake my head. "I don't think that will be appropriate, not to mention, the lady you were talking to Tuesday night might not like the fact that you're bathing another woman."

"Lady, on Tuesday?" I can tell he is trying hard to research the database of his memory. "In a silver car?"

I roll my eyes. "I guess it was a little dark." *I couldn't see the color because of my tears,* I want to say but refuse to give him that pleasure.

He starts laughing. "So that's why you haven't been answering my calls?"

"Scoop, I don't have time for games and I'm just...I want to get over Saturday night since it will never happen again."

"I don't know what gave you that idea, but anyway, that was my sister. She's my one and only biological sister, Shana. Macy, she was laughing at how you've been blowing me off. I ain't never had a woman see me calling and won't even answer the damn phone. To her, that is hilarious."

I look at him with my eyebrows furrowed. "I guess we both made assumptions, but unlike you, I wasn't bold enough to come into your space."

He smiles. "Maybe not, but whoever was up in here was getting ready to leave and never come back. Believe that."

"You haven't seen me all week so how do you figure you were going to throw someone out of my house. You are crazy for real." I start laughing and Scoop pulls me into his arms.

"Macy, listen, baby, I've been miserable. I couldn't under-stand why you stormed out of my spot, and then for you not to answer me almost made me blow my top. Baby, I just need you to be sure about me, Macy."

"What do you mean? I've been coming to your club an entire year. Many men have approached me and you've never seen me leave with not one. Didn't you know I was coming for you?"

"Listen, since we were in the sixth grade, me, John, and Philip promised each other that if the other was checking a girl out, she was off limits. We wouldn't approach her no matter how much we wanted her. Well, the night I took you in my office was the day I found out that you and John have never had anything. He made me believe you did."

"Wow! So that meant I was off limits?"

John is more of an ass than I thought.

CHAPTER 17
SHIT IN THE SHACK
JOSEPHINE

My baby summons me down to The Sugar Shack because he's sent Scoop to get his girl, and Scoop asked him to watch his place.

I walk in the door and before I can make it in good, P-baby makes long strides to stop me in my tracks.

"Baby, sit over there behind the bar with Tamika." She is one of The Sugar Shack's DJ's.

I smile and follow his instructions, but I see now this Negro is trying to make sure ain't nobody talking to me. Good thing is, both Macy and I are fond of Tamika. She's an around the way girl who is cooler than most pretty girls, because she doesn't know how beautiful she truly is.

"Well, hello, Mrs. Philip Micheals. I hear congratulations are in order."

I smile. "Yeah, he's swept me off my feet."

She gives me high five. "Philip is a good dude and so is Scoop. They just need to dump that damn no good ass John."

"Tamika, you feel that way too?"

"He's a jealous crawfish who pretends to be a part of their crew but his ass is envious as hell."

I nod as I look over toward John who was talking and laughing like he was the center of attention. But because I've seen envy in his eyes often, I agreed with Tamika. "You know Macy and I work for him and he's gotten worse over the years. He really was not like that at first."

Tamika looks at me. "I see you don't know, do you?"

"Know what?" I ask as she comes closer to where I am.

"When they were in high school, his momma was f'ing with this bottom boy thug and her boyfriend raped John. Ever since then, he's had problems getting women or keeping them because he's fighting feelings. Well, three years ago, they released the dude from jail for good behavior. John started going from bad to worse."

"Oh my God." I put my hand over my mouth. Macy and I always said he had a little sugar in his tank. I keep that to myself though.

She continues. "Going to jail and Scoop having to bail him out. Well, when he met Macy, he wanted to date her but never had the nerves to ask her to go out with him. So, instead of telling the truth, he had both Scoop and P-baby thinking Macy was cutting for him."

"Are you serious?" I act as if I didn't already know that part.

Tamika nods and puckers her lips.

I knew then I was about to get some good juice because anytime a sister nods and puckers, she's either about to go all deep in the business or she's calling out b-s.

"Yeah, and the guys have a pact to never undercut their friend by taking a lady they want. Well, from the first night Macy and you came into The Sugar Shack, she's been flirting with Scoop. And even though he liked her, he couldn't cross the line."

I laugh. "We were beginning to think he was gay." We both laugh.

"I can understand. So, on Saturday, one of the girls from the hood came up here. She was mad and ranting about trying to find John. Well, Scoop told her that John hadn't been here since Thursday. Come to find out, John and another dude in their business club were running a train on her and she sucked old boy, while John screwed her. Anyway, she starts itching, goes to the doctor, and finds out she had a venereal disease. She started telling Scoop that John and ole boy have been messing around for a year and they bring females in when they want to switch it up."

I turn my full body toward Tamika. "You gotta be kidding me!"

"I wish I were because I was sort of cutting for John. That shit disappointed me for real."

"Well, Tamika, he was raped and we all know that can mess with your mind. Maybe if he had a real woman who can look beyond that, he'd pick a side and stay there."

"Maybe or maybe not. I'm disappointed because he broke their friendship code. Had he not been lying, Scoop and Macy would have been together a long time ago. And also, had ole girl not come in the club Saturday, Scoop would still be upholding their pact. To me, John is not loyal. I could look over him f'ing a man given what happened to him, but I can't get over him f'ing over his friends."

I shake my head because she's the strongest woman I know. I'd rather him mess over his friends all day than to have his package up a negro's behind. "Well, Tamika, either way, I think we really need to pray for John."

"Somebody better because look who just walked through the door." Tamika nods and mouths 'that's her.' "Something is about to go down in The Sugar Shack."

I call out to P-baby because I can tell by the look in the woman's eyes that this wasn't about to be good. She looks a little on the rough side, but the huge black bag she carries just doesn't sit well with me. By the time P-baby makes it to the bar, the woman has made it to John.

It is like I am watching a bad movie that moves too quickly and I can't put the show on rewind, but I sure hear the shots. Pow! Pow! Pow! She shoots him three times and everyone scatters but P-baby.

My man jumps into action, grabbing the woman from behind, and wrestling her to the ground. I dial 911, and Tamika runs over to do CPR on John.

Heck! What just happened? I stand, shaking, watching the commotion of others. I can feel myself easing when I hear the sirens coming up the street. When the cops get her, and the gun, P-baby comes over and I fall in his arms.

By the time Tamika comes back to the bar, her clothes are covered in blood; John's blood. She is shaking like a leaf. P-baby gives me the keys to Scoops' office and asks me to take Tamika in there, help her shower, and get her one of Scoop's track suits from his closet.

I want to tell him, "Hell nawl, I just want to go home." But after my baby was as heroic as he was, I know I have to do whatever this man needs me to.

Now, isn't this some shit?

CHAPTER 18
HATE & SUGA DON'T MIX
MACY J & SCOOP

I look at him deeply because I can't believe what he's telling me.

Scoop reiterates. "Yes, baby, I've been watching you from the day I gave you my card to come to The Sugar Shack. Macy, I fell in love with you that day. Your soft gentle way, how you handle customers, and even how you say my name."

"You've got to be kidding me."

He rubs my arm. "No, I'm not. I watch how you are kind to men, but never let them get close. I see your moves, and I know you're a good lady."

I push him in his chest. "If you know that, then why didn't you come after me the other night?"

His face gets extremely serious and he asks, "Can I be honest?"

I nod. "Please do." My momma always told me it was the best policy.

"As much as I want you, Macy, I'm not willing to have partial parts of you. I have to know that you aren't lusting after me for sex, but that you are willing to love me enough to obey me as I obey Christ."

His response shocks me and I know he can see it by my facial expression. Finally I ask, "So, you are religious?"

He shakes his head. "No, I'm convinced."

Now he's thrown me by this. My mind is moving. "What do you mean by that?"

"I'm convinced that there is a God and that He's aligned a perfect plan that fits man. Now, some don't believe, but I do. I have a responsibility as a man to protect, love, guide, provide, cover, and commit to my wife. Macy, I can get sex from multiple women, and some of them will let me hit them at the same time. I know I'll be able to please my woman, but more importantly than pleasing her body, I want to love her unconditionally and help God cover her soul."

I look into his eyes and I can tell this is the language of his heart, mind, and soul. "I...I just have no words. I'm shocked because I never took you to be so deep. I'm honored, because you're sharing your heart with me. But I'm also heartbroken that you thought my needing you was just about my body. I too want a husband. I want everything you want to give, but I also want to be satisfied and never have to settle."

He pulls me between his legs as he unties the string on my robe. "Macy, you deserve everything your heart desires." Scoop lays his head on my stomach. "I want to lay my head here one day to feel my babies moving."

I rub his hair with my hand. It's the perfect moment and although my pussy thumping just as hard as it was Saturday, I make my mind satisfied with just being in his arms.

"Macy." He looks up at me. "Loving me isn't going to be easy. I deal with emotional trauma from PTSD. Some days I'm happy, other days I'm sad. And I pray everyday that no one makes me mad. It's the effect of being in Afghanistan for months at a time. I need you to know that along with my dick comes a life full of tragedy, loss, and love, but I'm willing to do everything I can to be the man God has called me to be."

I under eye him. "You're not a preacher, are you?" He laughs so hard at my expression until I start laughing but I'm dead serious.

"No, I'm not a preacher, but God has called me to love Him and my neighbor as myself. Which is why I didn't kick John's behind today. I gotta apologize for going ham on him too."

"He's a bit misunderstood, but there could never have been anything between him and I. His mother would drive me nuts."

Scoop laughs. "Yeah, she's a little pushy but she's trying to protect John the man since she failed to protect John the teenaged boy. I'll share that with you later. But since we are here, and you are as naked as a jaybird, how about letting me taste you?"

I rub his hair. "As enticing as that sounds, and as good as it would feel, I need to go get back in the tub and clean her. I wouldn't dare let you put your mouth on a nasty pussy. But you can kiss me."

"With pleasure." Scoop stands up, wraps his arms around me, pulls my naked body so close I can feel his cock bulging, and kisses me just as passionately as he did the first night he kissed me.

This feels good. And when his finger begins to roam until it finds my clit, I let him play with it because it's what I wanted. He rubs fast then slow, then fast again, and when I moan, he fingers me, while sucking on my breast, until I begin to call his name.

I am almost about to cum, when the ringing of his phone pauses our activity. I listen as he speaks with whomever is on the other end.

"Did what? Heck, no. Damn! Did he die? He's fighting for his life. I told that boy hate and sugar don't mix. Give us a moment and we'll be there soon." Scoop ends the call. "Baby, that was P. There's this chick John's been f'ing with and she's been looking for him. Well, she found him tonight at The Sugar Shack, and she shot him."

I look at him strangely. "Wait. Come again. My boss, John?"

"I'm sorry, Macy, but yes, that John. Do you want to go with me or do you want to stay here?"

I look at him with pure compassion. "I want to be wherever you are."

"Okay, go take a quick shower, I'll make a couple of calls, and I'll be waiting on you. Please try to hurry, baby, because I want to be at The Sugar Shack if the media comes up. This is our business and livelihood, and I don't need no crazy female f'ing up my place because she's mad."

"I understand and it won't take me long. I know his mother is going to be out of her mind." I leave Scoop and run to my room to grab my Nike tracksuit, some panties, a bra, and an undershirt. It is something I can throw on without ironing that will keep me warm in the hospital.

I pull the stopper to let out the bath water, but turn on the shower and wash my body as the water drains from the tub. Then it hits me, pray. "Father in the name of Jesus, I know I don't always have a clean mouth, but I try. Would you please protect John from death? Save him, Lord, in Jesus's name I pray."

That's the least I can do for a man who gave me a job all because he thought I had pretty eyes. He's trusted me and Jo with his baby, and just because he lied about me doesn't mean he didn't care for me. I finish and rush to the front room where Scoop is waiting for me, and we leave.

The escape is too big to ignore.

CHAPTER 19

THE SUGAR SHACK BLUES

By the time we make it to The Sugar Shack, WTBK News and other affiliates are on the lot, with lights on, and ready to get eyewitness accounts. They are too busy trying to interview patrons until Scoop and I are able to sneak in through his office door.

He goes to his desk and immediately calls his attorney and also has the police department to escort news reporters off his property.

No matter how angry John made him, he is still his friend and would never do anything to hurt his mother.

I hear sounds of muffled tears coming from the bathroom, so I knock. When I hear "Come in," I open the door. Josephine is holding a traumatized Tamika in her arms, rocking her like a baby, and praying.

I immediately go to their side. "Jo, we need to get her out of here."

"I know, Macy, but she's..."

"I know she's hurt and scared." I bend over to talk to her. "Tamika, what you did tonight probably has given John a chance to live. Listen, don't let the devil take the moment by

causing fear to hypnotize you. You are fearless. You are smart.
You have the power to trample over the enemy. And you have
friends."

Tamika starts to cry.

"Jo and I are going to be with you through this, but this
bathroom is nowhere you should stay. Let's go into Scoop's
office so we all can regroup. Are you ready?"

She nods.

Josephine and I help Tamika off the floor and we go into
Scoop's office and all sit on the sofa.

Josephine leans into me and whispers. "Thank you, friend,
and I promise you've missed your calling."

I laugh. I've never thought about it but I always have been
able to keep cool in the face of trouble. When you grow up
with a depressed mother, you learn how to talk people off
ledges. I just wish I would have never left my mother home
alone the day she died. Sometimes, I carry the guilt and weight
of her decision to take an overdose. By the time I finish talking
to her, Tamika is off the ledge and she's coming back to herself.

P-baby is giving Scoop the rundown on how everything
happened and Scoop is taking it all in. You can tell that they
both are affected by what happened but Scoop is a little more
angry than he is sad.

"Dude, you good. John's going to be good. I have faith in
God," P-baby tells his boy.

"I just hate that I wasn't here. You know, it's like the devil
will always try stuff when the parent is away. The Sugar Shack
is the closest thing I have to a child and I don't want it
destroyed because of this."

I chime in as I stand to go to his side. "Baby, everyone in
this town knows the reputation of The Sugar Shack. It's the
place where true adults come to relax, listen to old school and
beautifully made new age music. You can get a drink, meet
people, and when you leave, you always want to come back.

There's not a man or female in this town that can tarnish what you've created. Now, we will get through this, and we all will do it together."

"That part!" Josephine says as she points at me.

Scoop pulls me in his arms. I can tell it was refreshing for him to hear me say those words. Watching his eyes go from smoke gray to the lightest of gray tells me that a burden has been lifted from his shoulders.

"Okay, so what do I do next?" Scoop asked as though directing his question to the four of us.

After P-baby doesn't say anything, I chime in. "We let the clean-up crew finish cleaning The Sugar Shack. After they are finished, your head security guard can lock up. We, the five of us, should go to the hospital, show our support for John, and then go to my house so I can cook us all something to eat. The Sugar Shack blues can't live here or in our hearts. How does that sound?"

"It sounds marvelous to me and once they taste your cooking, they'll know it's a marvelous thing." Josephine laughs.

"Can she cook like that, baby?" P-baby asks Jo.

"Man, that girl cooks like a country grandma who has a husband and fifteen children. She throws down."

"Sounds good to me, baby." Scoop gets up from his seat and hugs me.

If I made the suggestion for any of us, it was for Tamika. I know that tonight, she has no business being alone. She has taken a hit trying to save the life of John, and no one had to tell me. It is the look in her eyes that I've seen time and time again. When she smiles, I know I suggested the right thing.

"Okay, so Tamika, I will drive your car to your house and Scoop can pick us up there. P-baby and Jo, meet us at my house and we can all ride in the big truck with you, P-baby. Is that all right?"

"Sounds perfect."

When we are all out of the building and getting into the cars, Scoop comes over to Tamika's car.

"Macy, I don't know what we would have done without you, baby. Thank you for everything."

I smile and whisper, "You can thank me later if you know what I mean."

"Girl, I've got you for the rest of your life and I'll be thanking you for a long time."

Things go exactly as planned. By the time we make it to the hospital, John has made it through his first surgery. I assure his mother that Josephine and I will make sure that all of the clients and the office are straight. And she really shows her appreciation by the long and tight hugs she gives us.

She is definitely the reason I prayed extra hard for John to pull through.

By the time we make it to my house, we all are tired and hungry. I make my famous fried chicken, a bowl of potato salad, some dirty rice, and some homemade rolls. Josephine insists that I make my momma's special kool-aid, and I do. Scoop drinks three glasses and I am happy that he loves it.

After dinner, and some good conversations, Tamika decides that she is going to let P-baby drop her back off to the hospital to be with John's mother. Josephine and I think that is all we need to prove that maybe, something is brewing in her heart for John deeper than even she imagines.

Scoop and I stand in my door, as if we lived together, and wave as our friends leave. Surely, this is going to be a wonderful year for all of us and life and love has really just begun.

It's about to be ON!

CHAPTER 20
SUGAR LIFE & SHACK LOVE
MACY J & SCOOP

I close the front door and Scoop locks it. Then I look at him with the slyest of smiles. "Okay, sir, I will see you tomorrow."

Scoop looks at me as if I'd lost my mind. "I wish I would go anywhere. Baby, please tell me I can stay."

"Oh, nawl, big man. You just talked noise and now you want to ask all sweet if you can stay. Hell nawl! It's time for you to shake my sugar shack."

"Come here." Scoop laughs and pulls me into his arms. "I knew you were special, Macy, but after tonight, I know just how special you are. I want you, no, I need you in my life."

I blush. "No, because I don't need you lusting after my pussy. See, you tasted my goods and now you are hooked on Macy. I want a man who will love and honor me, and only me, for the rest of his life. I want sex when I want it and how I want it. If I act like I just want the thang and not the man, give me what I want. If I want you to lick my vjay, and make me cum with your finger, that's what I want. If I want you to take me to church, and hang out with Josephine and I, then that's what I want. Can you handle all of my wants?"

Scoop laughs. "Girl, you are a mess, but yes, I can handle all of your wants and your needs. Now, can I stay?"

"It depends if you can start tonight giving me what I want."

He kisses me. "Okay, tell me what you want, Macy."

"Alexa, play "Sex Me" by Kelly."

I take Scoop by the hand and I lead him to my bedroom. My good mind is saying, "Wait," but...*Lord, forgive me because I have a debt to settle with this man.*

I dance all around him to the music, until I can see that he's fully aroused and ready for whatever. I push him to my bed and when he sits, I hit a button on my bedroom wall that causes the pole to come down. It's used for dancing and once it latches in place, I begin giving him a private show.

The show I've dreamt of giving him from the first day I laid eyes on him.

I thrust my pelvic, licking my tongue out, as I begin to throw my clothes off piece by piece. *I'm glad I put my sexy red panties and bra on.*

"It Seems Like You're Ready," by Kelly is the next song and it comes on at the right time. *I don't care what people say, his music is still my go to when I want to have the night of my life.* By the time he's watching the show with me in my bra and panties, his cock is standing at attention.

I crawl over to the bed, take off his shoes, socks, and then I stand, turn around, and roll my ass drop down in my catch-em-trap-em move, and he's caught. Scoop is watching me so hard I could have sworn I see slob fall from his mouth.

I dance back up, put my finger in my vjay and rub the juice from it on his lips.

He whispers, "Damn, Macy. What are you doing to me?"

I dance back up to him and take off his shirt as Ciara's "Body Party," comes on. Then I show him my dance skills. He can't tell me I'm not my altar ego that is part Ciara, part

Teyana. I dance until Scoop stands up and takes off his pants and his Polo underwear.

Yes! This man is well endowed. I say, "Alexa, play my Summer Walker's playlist."

"Girls Need Love" flows into the atmosphere as I walk up on him, and he is just as ready as I am to feel my touch as I am to feel his. I put some of the oil on my nightstand in my hand, and I stroke his cock up and down and use my other hand to cup and squeeze his testicles tenderly but enough to make him squirm. Then, I wrap my lips around the head and I pull it with just the right amount of force to make my lips pop.

The sound itself is driving him as much as the feeling of being swallowed and sucked with love and passion. This is the sugar life, in my shack of love, and I am not stopping until he is calling my name.

"Baby, baby," he moans.

"Say my name, say my name." I suck and pull, and lick, until he says, "Macy. F! Macy." I grin. *That's exactly what I wanted. To drive his ass crazy just like he did me.*

When I see he is at his breaking point, I mount him like a cowgirl on a prize winning bull. I work him until the sounds of my ass clapping together in sync with his moans and groans fills the air. When he bites his lip, I stop. It is like taking the toy from a man who is just beginning to love it. *He's got to pay for messing Macy J.*

I roll over on my back and say, "I've screwed you, now I need you to make love to me."

Scoop looks at me intensely. Then he mounts me, holding one of my legs firmly against his chest. *I can feel him so deep in me.* Now, it is my time to moan and groan. He moves slow but steady, and my vjay is playing a song all for the man who is making it wetter with every thrust.

"Scoop, Scoop," I moan and call his name.

"Oh you calling me now, huh?" He bites his lips, lowers my

leg, and holds my arms out with his hand in mine. This man is making sweet love to me, giving me sweet sugar in between our moans. Turning my home into our shack of love, and I am enjoying every second.

The minutes turn into hours, and we are still going at it like two starved for loving humans who land on an island with the one we want.

And when he tells me he is about to cum, I tell my body it's time.

I squeeze the walls of my vjay until my girl cups his cock and we sail into ecstasy.

I scream, he squeals, and shakes, and curses, and I know that this was the love I want for the rest of my life...but it isn't over yet.

After we shower, we lay together and just when he thought I was asleep, he decides it is time for him to get a taste of the vjay he claims as his.

And though I didn't mind at all, I know he has a score to settle and this sugar shack will be open all night. If this is what life with love feels like, I do not ever want anything less than this.

I dune opened a Scoop's box, but she's ready!

ABOUT THE AUTHOR

Ivory Keys is the pen name where this author explores steamy urban romances infused with Christianity, and about people living on their own terms that may or may not come to terms with living within the world's bubbles.

Unless you are looking for sweet and clean romances- you can read those under her pen name Danyelle Scroggins.

Learn more about her steamy urban and ratchet romances at www.authorivorykeys.com. You can also connect on any social media platforms with these icons.

facebook.com/authorivorykeys
instagram.com/authorivorykeys

Want to read Good Company for free? You can click HERE to join my mailing list and read GOOD COMPANY!